This book belongs to

_____

VOLUME **5**

POOH'S
NEW CLOTHES

WALT DISNEY FUN-TO-READ LIBRARY

A BANTAM BOOK
TORONTO • NEW YORK • LONDON • SYDNEY • AUCKLAND

Pooh's New Clothes   A Bantam Book/January 1986   All rights reserved.   Copyright © 1986 Walt Disney Productions.   This book may not be reproduced, in whole or in part, by mimeograph or any other means.
ISBN 0-553-05579-8

Published simultaneously in the United States and Canada.   Bantam Books are published by Bantam Books, Inc.   Its trademark, consisting of the words "Bantam Books" and the portrayal of a rooster, is Registered in U.S. Patent and Trademark Office and in other countries.   Marca Registrada.   Bantam Books, Inc., 666 Fifth Avenue, New York, New York 10103.   Printed in the United States of America   0 9 8 7 6 5 4 3 2 1

One day Pooh Bear was going to the bee tree to look for honey. On his way he saw a surprising thing. All of his friends were together in one place.

"Dear, dear!" said Pooh. "I wonder what is going on."

Then through the crowd he saw a fox.
"Who could he be?" Pooh wondered.
"Well, I'll just take a look and see!"

In the center of the crowd stood the handsome fox. The fox held up one beautiful outfit after another.

"Only someone who is very important would ever wear clothes like these. Take it from me, Sly Fox," said he.

All the animals nodded and agreed. You could tell just by his clothes that Sly Fox was important.

"With clothes like those, I could look big and brave," Piglet thought.

"Why, I could be the life of every party," thought Owl.

"They would make me feel almost happy," thought Eeyore.

"Where can I get some?" asked Tigger.

"Oh, do tell us, please," cried Kanga.

"I can make these clothes for you," said Sly Fox. "I have some of the best cloth ever made. No other cloth is as soft, as smooth, or as light. It is also magic cloth. Only <u>wise</u> people can see it."

"My word," muttered Owl.

"How wonderful," said Rabbit.

"Who will be the first to have clothes of magic cloth?" asked Sly.

"I will!" cried Pooh. "Do you think you could make a suit to fit me?"

"For a price, my good bear. For a price," said Sly, "I will make you a suit. But you must give me all of your honey."

"Hmm," thought Pooh. "That is quite a lot to ask."

"Wear it, and you will be the wisest bear around," said Sly.

"Oh, all right," sighed Pooh.

"It is a deal," cried Sly.

Sly Fox set up his shop in a quiet corner of the Wood. All the animals left him alone so that he could make Pooh's new clothes.

But Sly had played a trick on the good animals in the Hundred Acre Wood. There was no magic cloth at all! Day after day, Sly pretended to work. But all he really did was think about Pooh's delicious honey.

Meanwhile, Pooh Bear looked for his honey.

"Now where did I put those jars?" he sighed. "This is why I need magic clothes. They will turn me into a wise bear. Then I will always be able to find my jars of honey."

This thought pleased Pooh a lot. Now he
did not mind looking for the honey at all.

While Pooh looked for his honey, the other creatures in the Wood began to worry. "I do hope I will be able to see the clothes of magic cloth," Piglet said.

"Only wise people can see the clothes," said Owl. "I am sure that I will be able to see them."

"I know I will see them too," said Tigger. But he secretly wondered if he was wise enough.

"Maybe none of us is wise enough to see the magic cloth," thought Tigger. He was worried.

"Well, I am off," he said. Then he bounced on over to Sly's workshop. He wanted to find out if he was wise or not.

"Take a look," said Sly. "Isn't it lovely?"

"Uh-oh," thought Tigger. "I don't see anything at all!"

But that is not what Tigger said. He told Sly Fox it was the prettiest cloth he had ever seen. And he told the other animals the same thing.

Soon Owl began to wonder if <u>he</u> was wise enough to see the magic cloth. He did not want to be the only one who could not see it. So Owl, too, went to visit Sly.

"See here, wise Owl," said Sly. "Isn't my
cloth grand?"

Owl was about to say, "I don't see any
cloth." But he remembered that even Tigger
had seen it. "Yes, indeed. That cloth is
grand." He walked away slowly, thinking
very hard.

Next Piglet went to visit Sly Fox.

"Glad to see you, Piglet," said Sly. "Pooh's clothes look better every day."

But Piglet did not see any clothes. "Oh, dear," said Piglet in a worried voice. "I—I—just remembered something—something I must do at home!"

Piglet ran so fast he almost ran right
into Eeyore.

"Fine clothes," said Piglet nervously.
"Very fine clothes." He hurried away, shaking
his head.

Eeyore had heard quite enough about Pooh's magic clothes. "What good are magic clothes anyway?" he thought. "Besides, what if I am not wise enough to see them?" This thought made Eeyore very sad.

When he got to Sly's, Eeyore felt sadder than ever. "I <u>would</u> have to be the only one who cannot see Pooh's clothes!" he thought.

But Eeyore would not say that he could not see the clothes. So he muttered, "They are all right—if you like that kind of thing."

SLY FOX-TAILOR

Kanga and Roo also went to visit Sly.

"Oh, Mr. Fox! How lovely," said Kanga.

"What is Mama making such a fuss about?" wondered Roo. "I don't see any—" Roo began to say.

"Hush, dear," said Kanga. Then she left in a hurry.

"But Mama, there were no clothes in Mr. Fox's shop!"

"I know that, dear," answered Kanga. "Just don't tell anyone else."

The next day, Rabbit went to see Sly
Fox. He thought Sly might need some help.
Sly was happy to see Rabbit. "The
clothes are almost done," he cried. "Come
inside and take a look!"

Rabbit stepped into the shop. "There must be some mistake," he thought. "I do not see a stitch of clothing anywhere."

But all Rabbit said was, "My, my! Those clothes are wonderful, all right."

At last Pooh found all of his jars
of honey.
"Did Sly Fox say he wanted <u>all</u> of my
honey? Perhaps just <u>some</u> honey would do."

"He did say _all_ your honey jars, Pooh. But think of what you will get," said Piglet.

"The best clothes in all the world," added Rabbit.

"Yes, you are right," sighed Pooh. He picked up all his honey jars. "Here I go!"

"Yum!" thought Sly when he saw Pooh's honey. He grabbed the jars. "Here is your grand new suit."

"Ooh!" said Tigger

"Aah!" said Rabbit.

"But . . ." said Roo.

"Hush!" said Kanga.

SLY FOX - TAILOR

"I love them!" said Pooh. He did not care
that <u>he</u> could not see the clothes. He knew
he was just a bear of little brain. But Pooh
was glad that his wise friends could see
them. That was enough for him.

"See the pretty flowers on the shirt?" asked Sly. "They look so real that you can almost smell them."

As Pooh sniffed the air, Sly pretended to
help Pooh put on his new shirt and pants.
"Pretty good fit, aren't they? Now for the
jacket," said Sly. "A beautiful suit. And it is
so light in weight that you won't even know
you are wearing it!"

"That's true," said Pooh in a small voice.

"How do I look?" asked Pooh.

"Handsome," said Kanga.

"Brave," said Piglet.

"Happy," said Eeyore.

"Not wise?" asked Pooh Bear.

"Oh yes, very wise," added Tigger. He was glad to be able to say something nice.

"That's just what I thought," said Pooh.

TAILOR

Just then Pooh saw Christopher Robin.
"What do you think of my new clothes,
Christopher Robin?" asked Pooh.

"Why Pooh, you silly bear. Those are the same clothes you always wear," said Christopher Robin.

"But I gave Sly Fox all of my honey to make these. They are made from magic cloth. Only wise people can see them—" Pooh stopped.

Suddenly Pooh Bear knew the truth. There was no one wiser than Christopher Robin. If he could not see the clothes, they just were not there.

"That Sly Fox played a trick on me," he said. "I wish I had kept a little honey. It helps to have honey at a time like this."

"Don't feel bad, Pooh. Sly Fox tricked us all," said Owl.

"I knew there was no cloth," said Roo.

"All of you knew," said Christopher Robin, "but you were afraid to believe your own eyes. You were afraid of what the others would think. But I think you are all perfect just the way you are."

Then Christopher Robin took them home.
And he gave Pooh Bear an extra hug to
show him he was the best bear in the whole
wide world.